THE·LAND·OF
NOD

THE
BLACK
MOUNTAIN

THE
FLOATING
ISLES

SNOWY
VILLAGE

ENCHANTED
VALLEY

CREEPY
CASTLE

GLOOMY
DEN

BOULDER
GORGE

GLITTER
BAY

For Amelie, Ned and Eleanor
R.F.

For Mam
C.C.

LADYBIRD BOOKS

Ladybird Books is part of the Penguin Random House group of companies
whose addresses can be found at global.penguinrandomhouse.com.

www.penguin.co.uk   www.puffin.co.uk   www.ladybird.co.uk

Penguin
Random House
UK

First published 2018
023
Written by Rhiannon Fielding. Text copyright © Ladybird Books Ltd, 2018
Illustrations copyright © Chris Chatterton, 2018
Moral rights asserted
Printed in China
A CIP catalogue record for this book is available from the British Library
ISBN: 978–0–241–34892–5
All correspondence to:
Ladybird Books, Penguin Random House Children's
One Embassy Gardens, 8 Viaduct Gardens, London SW11 7BW

TEN MINUTES TO BED

Little Unicorn

Rhiannon Fielding • Chris Chatterton

Twinkle the naughty unicorn
had glittery feet and a sparkly horn.
"Ten minutes to bed!" her dad would call –

but this little unicorn . . .

was **not tired** at all!

Unicorns live in a **magical** land,
full of marshmallow clouds and pink sugar sand.
"Nine minutes to bed – let's try to be quiet – "
But Twinkle was causing . . .

a bit of a riot!

Now, unicorns don't often cause **trouble,**
but Twinkle always seemed to make double.
"**Eight minutes to bed!**" Her daddy frowned –

but Twinkle

was dancing . . .

and **prancing** around!

Dashing about, chasing pixies and sprites,
and fairies that fluttered like tiny bright lights.
"Seven minutes!" said Dad, but she swished her tail,
for Twinkle had found . . .

a
footprint
trail.

"What sharp claws, and what huge feet!
I wonder what **hairy trolls** like to eat!"
"Six minutes to bed," said her dad with a sigh –

but NOW Twinkle
had spotted . . .

bright wings
in the sky!

A baby dragon, swooping higher and higher, breathing great flames of golden fire!

"Five minutes to bed, so don't go far . . ."
but Twinkle had seen . . .

a shooting star!

As it shot through the sky like a spark,
she followed the star's bright silver arc.
"Four minutes," she grumbled, with a big groan –
but soon she'd forgotten . . .

how to get home.

In the **magical** velvety starlit night,
Twinkle scrunched her eyes up tight.
"**Three minutes,**" she thought – her bedtime was near,

so she wished . . .

and she wished . . .

and a **rainbow** appeared!

From a unicorn's wish, a rainbow is made,
so no little unicorn's ever afraid;
and if a unicorn's lost and alone
they follow their rainbow . . .

to lead them back home!

Over the rainbow, back through the wood,
Twinkle **trotted** as fast as she could.
"Two minutes to bed!" she heard her dad call.
Perhaps she was ready . . .

for bed, **after all!**

Curled up tight, feeling happy and warm.
"So snug!" thought the sleepy unicorn.
"There you are, Twinkle! One minute to bed . . ."

But Twinkle . . .

. . . was **fast asleep,** instead.

THE·LAND·OF
NOD
THE BLACK MOUNTAIN
THE FLOATING ISLES
SNOWY VILLAGE
ENCHANTED VALLEY
CREEPY CASTLE
GLOOMY DEN
BOULDER GORGE
GLITTER BAY
N
W
E
S

THE
ANCIENT FOREST

OUTER
SPACE

EMERALD
GLEN

DEADLY
CREEK

GIANTS' TOWN

THE
STINKY
SWAMPS

GOLDEN
COVE

RICKETY
BRIDGE